The Peanut Pickle

The Peanut Pickle

A Story about Peanut Allergy

Written by Jessica Jacobs
Illustrated by Jacquelyn Roslyn

Sky Pony Press
New York

Sky Pony Press books may be purchased in bulk at special discounts for sales promotion, corporate gifts, fund-raising, or educational purposes. Special editions can also be created to specifications. For details, contact the Special Sales Department, Sky Pony Press, 307 West 36th Street, 11th Floor, New York, NY 10018 or info@skyhorsepublishing.com.

Sky Pony® is a registered trademark of Skyhorse Publishing, Inc.®, a Delaware corporation.

Visit our website at www.skyponypress.com.

10 9 8 7 6 5 4 3 2 1

Manufactured in China, May 2012
This product conforms to CPSIA 2008

Library of Congress Cataloging-in-Publication Data is available on file.

ISBN: 978-1-61608-672-5

Disclaimer: The information contained herein is not intended to be a substitute for professional medical advice. The publishers, author, and illustrator cannot accept any responsibility for any action taken or injury incurred as a result of any information contained within this book. Please seek the advice of your physician with regards to your food allergies.

For Grant and Hope

My name is Ben, and I am six years old. I'm like other kids except I can't eat peanuts or peanut butter. I can't even touch them. That's because I'm allergic to peanuts. When I was two, I took a bite of peanut butter and got really sick. My lips got puffy, and I got a rash all over. I couldn't breathe and had to go to the hospital.

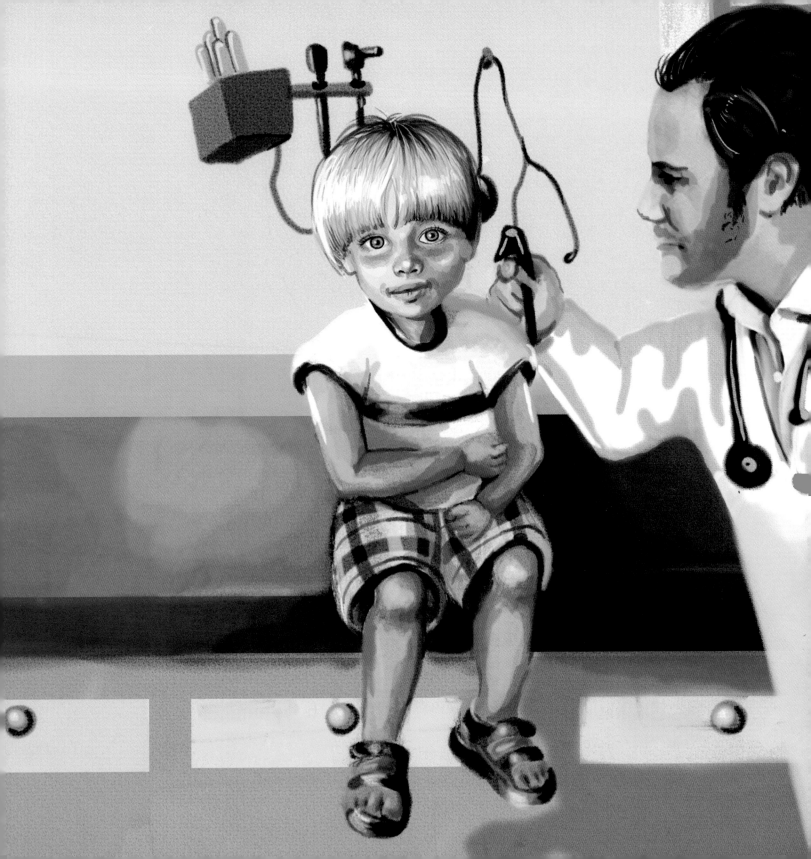

I don't want to get sick like that again. To stay safe, I have to be very careful about what I eat and ask people not to eat peanuts or peanut butter when they are with me. Sometimes it's hard to tell others about my food allergy. Sometimes I am scared to talk, but I take a deep breath and do it anyway. I always feel better after I speak up.

One day, my mom and I
picked up my friend Brandon
at his house. We were going to
the park. He had a bag
of snacks with him.
Before we even pulled
out of the driveway,
we found out what
was in the bag.

You guessed it: peanuts!
I said, "Brandon, will you leave those peanuts at home? I'm allergic and will get sick if I touch them."

"I don't want you to get sick," he said. "I'll be right back!" He walked back to his house and handed them to his mom.

Another time, I was talking to my cousin on the phone. She and her family were getting ready to come over and visit us that afternoon. She said they were bringing peanut butter and jelly sandwiches over to our house for lunch.

"Sarah, I am allergic to peanuts. Would you leave those sandwiches at home?" I asked.

"Oh, yes," Sarah answered, "I'm sorry, Ben, I forgot."

At our house, my mom helped us make homemade pizza for lunch. Sarah said it was the best pizza she'd ever had.

Last Christmas, my Aunt Carly brought over homemade cookies. They looked delicious, but I didn't know if they were safe for me. "Do any of those have peanuts in them?" I asked. "If they do, they'll have to stay in your car. I have a peanut allergy."

My aunt said they had no peanuts or peanut butter in them. She had remembered about my peanut allergy and wanted me to be safe. She had made my favorite butter cookies. I love my Aunt Carly!

I play on a T-ball team. It's my favorite sport. One of my teammates brought peanut butter granola bars to practice to share with the team. I knew I couldn't stay and play ball if the other kids started eating them.

"Adam," I said, "I'm allergic to peanuts. It wouldn't be safe for me to stay at practice if everyone was eating peanut butter granola bars. Can you hand them out after practice, after I go home?"

"Sure, I don't mind waiting," Adam said.

We all had lemonade during practice instead of a snack.

At Easter, my grandma brought over some candy for me. I like candy, but I have to be careful about what kind I eat. "Are there peanuts in it?" I asked. My grandma said she didn't know. There were no ingredient labels on the candy.

"I can't eat food without an ingredient label," I told her. "My mom and dad always check the label before I eat something. Without it, we don't know what's in the candy."

My grandma said she was sorry and that next Easter she would bring me a toy instead. That sounded great to me!

One time at school, a girl in my class brought cupcakes for her birthday. When she started to hand one to me, I said, "Teresa, I can't eat those. I have a peanut allergy."

"These are chocolate, not peanut butter," she said.

"Sometimes food can have little bits of peanut in it," I told Teresa. "I can't eat food unless my mom or dad says it's okay. I have a special snack that Mrs. Hardy is getting."

My teacher keeps a bag of safe snacks for me so I always have something to eat while the other kids eat their treats.

My family and I went to a pool party in the summer. When we got there, we saw bowls of peanuts sitting on all the tables. Lots of people were already there and had been eating them. It wasn't a safe place for me to be, so we had to leave. I was sad because we couldn't stay.

It looked like a fun party, and I really wanted to swim. But there were just too many peanuts around! Instead, we went to a park and played at the playground and had a picnic lunch. It turned out to be a fun day after all!

One day, my neighbors came over to play. I really wanted to play, but Max was eating a snack and had peanut butter all over his hands and face.

I said, "I can't play with you right now. Max has peanut butter all over him, and I'm allergic to it. Can you come back later, when he's all cleaned up? We can play

"C'mon, Max, let's go home
and have Mom wash you up,"
said Julia. "Then we can play

I go to lots of different places. If there is food, I have to ask what's in it. If someone is eating food near me, I have to find out what it is. I stay away from peanuts and peanut butter. I don't want to get sick again.

My peanut allergy is a part of me. It goes with me wherever I go. And that's okay. People who care about me want me to stay safe and healthy. I care about myself, too.

If you have a peanut allergy, remember these rules:

1. Always check food labels before eating any food.

2. Carry your EpiPen® with you at all times.

3. Wear your medical alert bracelet.

4. Do not eat food if you don't know what's in it.

5. If you eat something and feel sick, tell an adult right away.

Note to parents:

Peanut allergies among children are growing at an alarming rate. The reason for this increase is unclear. Approximately 1 percent of the U.S. population (roughly 3 million people) is allergic to peanuts and/or tree nuts. It is important to remember that this is a potentially life-threatening, and usually lifelong, condition. Very few children outgrow their allergy to peanuts. Prevention and planning are necessary to help prevent an accidental ingestion.

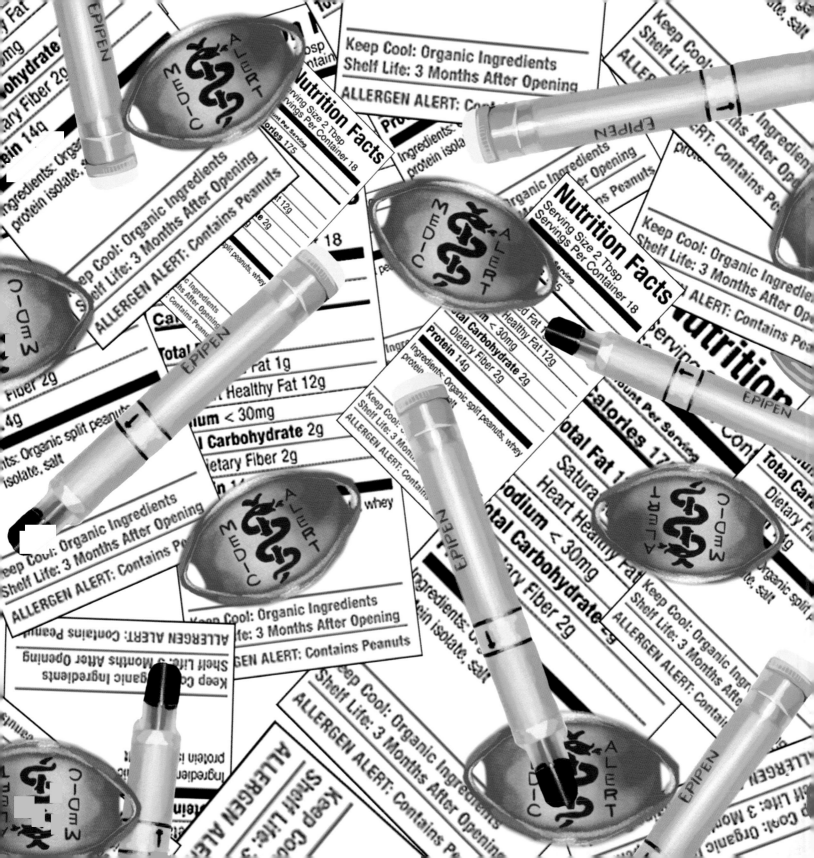

Refer to the following guidelines to help decrease your child's risk of reaction:

1. Always read food labels on everything before you allow your child to eat.

2. Have your child's EpiPen® and antihistamine with him/her at all times.

3. If you are not with your child, make sure a responsible adult knows the signs of an allergic reaction and how to treat it.

4. Have an emergency plan in case of accidental ingestion.

5. Teach your child not to accept food from others without your approval.

6. Do not allow your child to eat foods from bakeries or Chinese restaurants. The chance for cross-contamination is very high in these places.

7. Educate yourself on food allergies and stay informed.